Under the Night Sky

Amy Lundebrek
Illustrated by Anna Rich

TILBURY HOUSE, PUBLISHERS
Gardiner, Maine

I snuggle under the covers, and Ms. Gallo from across the hall clicks my apartment door shut. I get in my bed when she tells me to, but I won't go to sleep until my mama comes home. I never do.

When Mama is here, the door will creak open. I'll hear her keys clink as she sets them on the shelf. One by one, her boots will thunk on the mat, and she'll sigh. She always does.

Then I'll hear her footsteps and see a light under my door. That's my cue to shut my eyes and pretend I've been asleep. She'll cross my room and bend down to kiss me. She'll smell like the grease from the factory. She usually kisses my cheek and says, "Goodnight, my little bear."

That's when I'll go to sleep.

But instead, I hear a pounding up the stairs, and the door to our apartment flies open so hard it smacks the wall with a loud bang. I don't hear her keys or her boots, or her sigh. I sit upright in my bed gasping for air until I hear my mama's voice. "Get your boots! Get your jacket! Put on your hat and mittens!"

My hands are shaking while I put on my jeans. She sounds excited, but where are we going?

"Mama, what's wrong?" I call out from my room.

"Nothing's wrong," she says.

"Then where are we going?" I ask.

Her face pokes around my door. The light streams in, and I blink my eyes. She is smiling, so my hands don't shake anymore. She tosses my hat to me.

When I am mostly bundled up, Mama pulls me by the hand through our apartment. She is so excited she almost pulls me though the door in sock-feet. I pull back a little and look down at my boots.

"Boots!" she says, and stops so I can put them on.

Ms. Gallo is on the landing with her two boys and girl. They look sleepy, and Kevin is missing one of his mittens. Ms. Gallo and Mama nod to each other.

"Where are we going?" says Kevin.

"You'll see," says Ms. Gallo. Kevin looks at me and shrugs.

We all hustle down the stairs. I'm in the lead, so I push the heavy glass door open. That first breath of icy cold stings my throat. My breath hangs in front of me like a wintry ghost. Our boots sound crunchy in the snow.

In the big parking lot, there are other people standing around. Some are sitting on their cars. The old lady and man who live on the first floor are sitting in the front seat of their white minivan.

"Is there a fire?" I ask. "I didn't hear the fire alarm."

We've reached our old
Mercury, and Mama digs
around in the back seat. I move
to get in, but she shuts the
door before I have a chance.
She spreads out a wool army
blanket on the hood.

"Everybody up," she says.
Ms. Gallo's kids and I crawl
up on the hood.

"I think our moms have
gone crazy," whispers Kevin.

"Ready?" says my mama.

We all nod, but we look
around at each other still
wondering what's going on.

"Okay, look up!" Mama
points above our heads.

I never knew the sky could be so big.

I stand up on the hood of our car to drink it up. There are colors moving, taking up the whole sky in red and green and white. Then I realize that all the people in the parking lot are looking up. Even the old lady and man in their minivan are straining to look up at the sky through their front windshield.

Everyone is silent.

Sometimes the colored lights flash; here one moment, there the next. Sometimes they change shape slowly, like clouds, so I don't realize the picture has changed until it's done. Sometimes the color oozes from one part of the sky to the other. The lights twist like colored ropes. They flicker like colored flames.

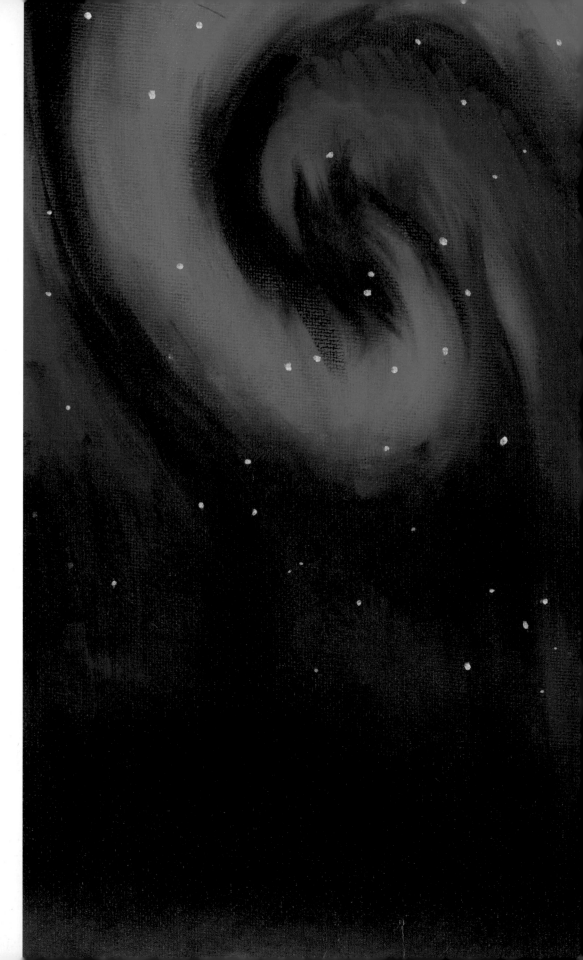

Mama turns to me and looks into my eyes. She and I are smiling together.

She whispers to me. "It's a good night, isn't it?"

I nod.

Then Mama says, "When you get older, you and I might disagree about some things."

I don't know how to answer her.

"You don't have to say anything," says Mama. "Just remember tonight. Remember these lights, how they dance. And if you ever feel angry that I'm not letting you have your way, remember that I'm on your side. I promise I will always try to give you the best things in life."

As fast as the talk had started, it's over, and Mama is laughing deep and loud with Ms. Gallo again.

I look up at the building, at my bedroom window. Mama woke me up just to share this with me.

People who have been standing alone in the parking lot are now wandering toward Mama and Ms. Gallo. They are all chatting about the rare lights in the sky.

"It's the solar wind hitting the earth's magnetosphere," whispers Kevin. He knows these kinds of things. I sit down by him. I think about a strange wind from the sun hurtling toward the earth like a Chinese dragon spewing flames into our night sky.

"Have you seen it before?" I ask him.

"Once, when we were driving home from my great aunt's house," he says.

"Was it the same as tonight?"

"No. That time it was fast. The lights licked up into the sky on the horizon, all different colors, and then they were gone," he says. "Our family has been waiting ever since then to see them again."

Almost everyone in the parking lot has gathered around our old Mercury. They are talking about things like rent money and the price of gas.

A little boy in a striped hat is wandering among the adults. I think I might have teased him at the bus stop once. I pat the hood in front of me. He hops up next to us, and I ask him his name.

My neck starts to hurt
from tilting my head to the
sky, so I rest my back against
the coolness of our car. The
cold soaks through the blanket.
It soaks through my jacket
and my jeans, but Kevin and
the other kids are pressed close
around me, and I feel their
warmth. We watch the lights
in the sky.

They flash and flicker,
jab and duel, dance and whirl.
Sometimes the sky seems to
split in two with the white
lights on one half and the
red on the other. The green
hovers on the horizon and
then splashes the two halves
together. I think I see flashes
of blue.

The lights curl, and then
pause. Sometimes they pause
so long I think they are gone.
But then they burst and splash
the sky again.

They whirl, and we watch.
They flicker, and we watch.
They dance, and we watch.
Ever so slowly, I am whirled
and flickered and danced into
the darkness of the sky and
the twinkling stars.

I wake up with my head wrapped in the colors of my dream. Was it a dream?

No, there are my mittens and hat on the floor beside my bed. I am still wearing my jeans. I look out my window at the gray morning light. The colors, if they were really there, are gone now.

Mama pokes her head around my door, ready to wake me up. That's when I'm sure we really saw them. This morning, I see those lights are still dancing in my mama's eyes.

Tilbury House, Publishers
8 Mechanic Street
Gardiner, Maine 04345
800–582–1899 • www.tilburyhouse.com

First hardcover edition: June 2008 • 10 9 8 7 6 5 4 3 2 1

To Ryan Lundebrek for his encouragement and support. —AL

To Otto and Harry, love always. —AR

Library of Congress Cataloging-in-Publication Data
Lundebrek, Amy, 1975-
Under the night sky / Amy Lundebrek ; illustrated by Anna Rich. — 1st hardcover ed.
    p. cm.
Summary: A boy is surprised when his mother tells him to get up and dressed when she returns
from work late one night, but soon they are outside, surrounded by neighbors, watching an
amazing display of the northern lights.
ISBN 978-0-88448-297-0 (hardcover : alk. paper)
[1. Auroras—Fiction. 2. Neighbors—Fiction. 3. Single-parent families—Fiction. 4. Mothers
and sons—Fiction.] I. Rich, Anna, 1956- ill. II. Title.
PZ7.L97883Und 2008
[Fic]—dc22
                                2007043344

Designed by Geraldine Millham, Westport, Massachusetts
Printed and bound by Sung In Printing, South Korea